My Grampa's Got
BIG pockets.

My Grampa's Got BIG Pockets

Selina Young

M

PAN MACMILLAN
CHILDREN'S BOOKS

In memory
of
Alex and Edward.

First published 1993 by Pan Macmillan Children's Books
This Picturemac edition published 1994 by Pan Macmillan Children's Books
a division of Pan Macmillan Publishers Limited
Cavaye Place London SW10 9PG
and Basingstoke

Associated companies throughout the world

ISBN 0-333-59315-4

1 3 5 7 9 8 6 4 2

A CIP catalogue record for this book is available from
the British Library

Printed in Hong Kong

On Sundays, Roxanne would visit her
grandparents. In the afternoon she would go
into the garden and watch Grampa gardening.
If it was cold or rainy they would stay indoors
and Grampa would tell Roxanne about his days
as a sailor and his life on the open sea.

Grampa was really good at telling stories. But he
wouldn't begin without first looking in his big
pockets (where he kept a lot of interesting
things). On this Sunday, Roxanne sat and
waited while he rummaged about,
until he produced a small glass
bottle with a small sailing
boat inside it.

"Babbling baboons! If it isn't our old ship,"
said Grampa. "I can remember that
shipwreck as if it were yesterday . . ."
And Roxanne knew that they were off
on another adventure.

As she listened she saw that Grampa had
become a handsome hero, captain of the
sinking ship, and she was his able seagirl. She
could smell the salty sea and hear the crashing
waves.

Grampa (the brave hero) was
clinging to some wreckage, the
ship's cat and the captain's parrot
were perched on a barrel and
Roxanne (the able seagirl) had
somehow managed to stay afloat.

In the distance, she could see the lifeboats
pulling away and beyond them, on the far
horizon, loomed the sinister black shape of a
pirate ship.

Try as she would, Roxanne could not stop
herself drifting towards it – until she was so close
that the evil pirates reached down, pulled her
out of the water and tied her to the mast.

Meanwhile, the handsome hero (and the cat and the parrot) had sneaked on board to rescue her. But unfortunately, after a rather tricky sword fight with our hero, they too were captured and all of them were made to walk the plank.

Even though our hero was very handsome, he wasn't a good swimmer. Just as it seemed that all was lost, a great fountain of water burst through the waves and up came a huge blue whale. The whale – who had been having a nap on the seabed – gave a great yawn.

"Jump!" called our hero: and that's what they all did, straight into the whale's mouth and down into her stomach.

Off went the whale – flicking her tail and
accidentally making the pirate ship do a
somersault into the air (serve those pirates
right!).

Fortunately for the fearless sailors the whale was a friendly sort and once they were in her stomach she offered to take them back to shore. The sailors sat crunching mint humbugs and eating ship's biscuits (which were all salty and soggy from the shipwreck) as they planned their next move: to return home before tea.

brain

A Big Kir heart

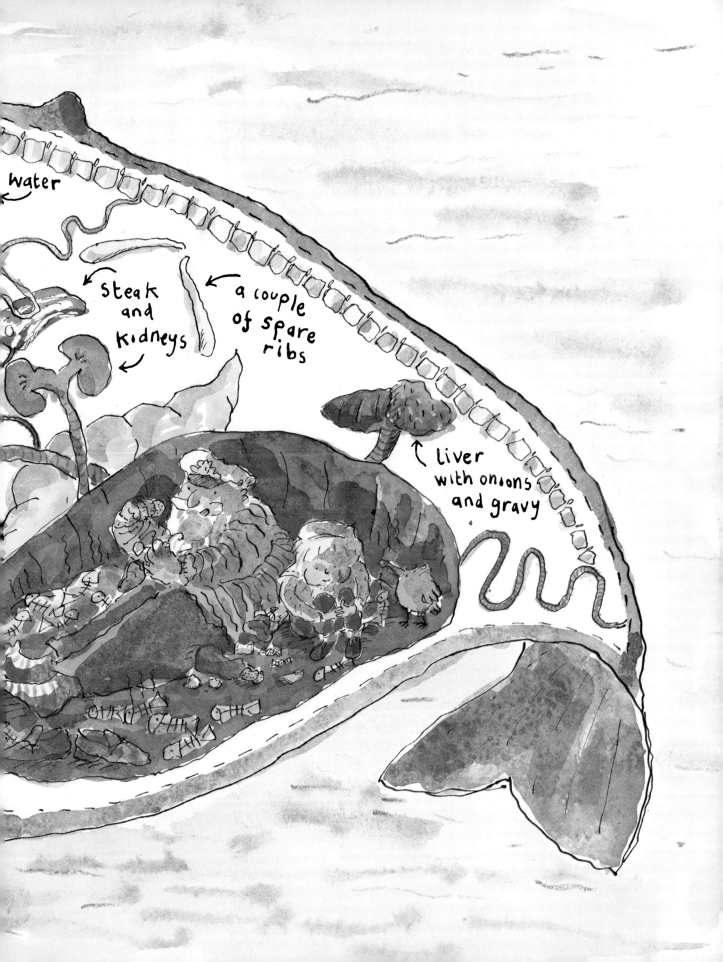

When the whale reached the shore, she politely
spat them out and then dived back down to the
seabed (after she had swum out a bit so as not to
knock her head on the bottom).

They landed with a bump. When they had
brushed themselves off, the handsome hero
rummaged once more in his pocket. He found
a little silver whistle, took it out and gave it to
the able seagirl. She blew it very hard –

WHEEEEEEEEEET

There in front of them appeared a big yellow bus (the able seagirl was *very* surprised, and so was the handsome hero, but he didn't show it).

It was crammed full of animals on their way home from school. Luckily our hero had remembered his bus pass and they managed to get on (though the ship's cat had to travel with the luggage). They felt sure they would be home in time for tea now.

Just when they were sitting back and thinking
of hot buttered toast and Grama's fruit cake, the
big yellow bus got stuck between two rocks. Even
the elephants couldn't move it. Would the
shipwrecked sailors ever get home?

The able seagirl was determined to find a way.
She explained to the eldest elephant that they
had been shipwrecked and captured by pirates
and swallowed by a huge whale and all they
wanted was to be home in time for tea. So the
elephant (who was very kind) said he would
take them home on his back.

The seagirl took one enormous leap and landed on the elephant's back. Off they went through the jungle, slowly at first and then quite fast. As they went, things crashed and banged all around (he was clumsy, you see). He made so much noise that Grama came to see what all the fuss was.

"Don't worry, Grama," said Roxanne, the able seagirl, "I'm coming to the table on my elephant." And Grampa winked at her (the wink of a handsome hero).

the End.

P.S. Those Pirates managed to swim to a little deserted Island do you think someone should Rescue Them?
K

Available in Macmillan hardback:

Grampa Goes West Selina Young

Other Picturemacs you will enjoy

Mucky Moose Jonathan Allen

Hurry Up, Franklin Paulette Bourgeois / Brenda Clark

Nellie's Knot Ken Brown

Jake and the Babysitter Simon James

Tacky the Penguin Helen Lester / Lynn Munsinger

The Wizard, The Fairy and the Magic Chicken Helen Lester / Lynn Munsinger

If Dinosaurs were Cats and Dogs Colin McNaughton

Elizabeth and Larry Marilyn Sadler / Roger Bollen

Say Hello, Tilly! Wendy Smith

For a complete list of Picturemac titles write to
Pan Macmillan Children's Books
18–21 Cavaye Place
LONDON
SW10 9PG